P9-DEQ-390

Duck & Company Christmas

Kathy Caple

Holiday House / New York

To the memory of my good friend
Ellen Weiss

HOLIDAY HOUSE is registered in the U.S. Patent and Trademark Office.
Printed and Bound in May 2011 at Tien Wah Press, Johor Bahru, Johor, Malaysia.
The text typeface is Family Dog Fat.
The artwork was created on Arches 140 lb hot pressed watercolor paper
using gouache and ink.
www.holidayhouse.com
First Edition
1 3 5 7 9 10 8 6 4 2

Library of Congress Cataloging-in-Publication Data
Caple, Kathy.
Duck & Company Christmas / by Kathy Caple.—1st ed.
p. cm.
Summary: Duck and Rat's bookstore is busy as Christmas
approaches and all the animals buy gifts and celebrate
with their friends.
ISBN 978-0-8234-2239-5 (hardcover)
[1. Animals—Fiction. 2. Christmas—Fiction.]
I. Title. II. Title: Duck and Company Christmas.
PZ7.C17368Dv 2011
[E]—dc22
2010029574

Contents

1. The Display

Duck put the last gumdrop

on the gingerbread house.

"It's our best window display ever," said Duck.

"It looks good enough to eat."

"It should be," said Rat.

"It is made of cookies, candy, and frosting."

"I can't wait to see it from the sidewalk,"

said Duck.

He went outside.

The gingerbread house had a warm glow
in the window.

Duck looked up and down the street.

Everywhere, stores were decorated

for Christmas.

The only problem was the rain.

"What we need is snow," said Duck.

"We could decorate the store with
paper snowflakes," said Duck
when he got back inside.
"That will put everyone in a
holiday spirit."
"Don't expect me to cut out
a bunch of dumb snowflakes," said Rat.
He had been crabby all day.
Duck had a better idea.

2. Paper Snowflakes

Duck made a sign.

HELP CUT OUT
PAPER SNOWFLAKES!

GET FREE COCOA.

WIN A PRIZE!

Before long the store
was filled with customers.

Everyone was sipping cocoa
and snipping paper.
"There should be a prize for the most
snowflakes cut," said Frog.
"I've already cut out ten."
"Rat and Duck should give a prize
for the best snowflakes too,"
said Mother Hen.

"This whole thing is dumb," said Badger.
"Duck and Rat should pay us for doing this."

Badger folded
some paper.
He snipped
and thought.
Then he snipped
some more.

He turned the paper this way and that.
He made a few more cuts.
Finally he opened the snowflake.

Badger smiled.
"Ahh!" said Duck.
"Wow!" said
everyone else.

Badger was very happy with his prize.
Rat was very happy with all the snowflakes.

3. All Wrapped Up

Squirrel walked in with two large bags.

They were filled with wrapping paper,

tape, and ribbon.

"Excuse me," said Squirrel.

"I need a job as a gift wrapper.

I just quit Burt's Department Store.

The customers were all cranky.

I even brought my own supplies."

"In that case, you're hired," said Duck.

"You can start right away."

"Oh, goodie," said Squirrel.

Her first customer was Weasel.

"This book is for Aunt Fleecy," said Weasel.

"She is very fussy."

Squirrel took out snowflake paper.

"Not snowflakes!" said Weasel.

"Aunt Fleecy hates snow.
  Use the red paper."

Squirrel rolled out
the red paper.

"No. Make that green
  paper with sparkles,"
said Weasel.

Squirrel wrapped
Aunt Fleecy's book
in green paper
with sparkles.

"Hey, that paper is too
wrinkly. And don't use
so much tape,"
said Weasel.
"Use ribbon instead."

Squirrel cut a
strand of gold ribbon.
"Not gold ribbon.
Use silver ribbon."

Squirrel made a bow.
"That bow is too big,"
said Weasel.

Squirrel made
a smaller bow.
"Now it's
too small,
and watch out
for the—"

Squirrel grabbed a big sheet
of tissue paper.
She threw it
over Weasel
and tied it
around his knees.

17

"Wrap it yourself,"
said Squirrel.

"I know," said Weasel.
"I will give *myself* as a present
to Aunt Fleecy.
And I will keep the book."
Weasel opened his umbrella
and left the store.

4. The Gingerbread House

Mother Hen walked into the store
with Little Peep.

"I need a book for Uncle Gizzard.

I need one for Auntie Comb too."

Duck and Rat got busy helping Mother Hen.

Little Peep looked at
the gingerbread house.
She took a cookie
from the trim
and ate it.

Little Peep got
inside the house.
She licked off the
frosting.
Little Peep
ate and ate.

"Shopping is over,"
said Mother Hen
as Squirrel wrapped
the presents.
Little Peep scurried
out of the house.
She hopped
to the floor.
She opened
a book.

"Look at what
a good reader
Little Peep is,"
said Mother Hen.
"I'll buy this book too."

Later that afternoon,

Squirrel looked at the gingerbread house.

Something did not look right.

"I will even out the trim,"

said Squirrel.

She took a cookie

and ate it.

"Much better," she said.

Rat walked past the gingerbread house.

He ate a row of candy wafers.

Duck came along.

"I'll just have a little taste," said Duck.

He pulled off a gumdrop.

CREAK!

CRASH!

The whole house fell down.

"I don't understand," said Duck.

"I only ate one gumdrop."

Rat made a sign.

FREE
GINGERBREAD
WHILE
SUPPLY
LASTS!

RUMBLE, RUMBLE.

The hockey team passed through.

"Look! Free cookies. Yum!"

Rat and Duck looked at the tray.

"All gone" was all they said.

5. Snow

"Hey, everyone," said Skunk.

"I smell snow!"

"It's just paper," said Squirrel.

"The snowflakes are made of paper."

"Not those," said Skunk. "Real snow.

Come out and take a whiff."

Everyone ran outside.

They all sniffed the air.

The air smelled cold.

They looked at the sky.
The sky was gray.
They listened.
Everything was
absolutely quiet.

"Now close your eyes and think *snow*,"
said Skunk.

Just then a snowflake landed on Rat's nose.

It was followed by another, and another.

"I told you I smelled snow," said Skunk.

6. Christmas Eve

The next morning there was snow everywhere.

When Duck and Rat got to the store,
customers were already arriving.
"Today is Christmas Eve," said Frog.
"I still need to buy one more present."

More customers came and went.

By noon the wind picked up.

All afternoon it snowed hard.

By closing time it was snowing so hard,
they could barely see out the window.

"We'd better stay in here until it blows over,"
said Duck.

Squirrel turned up
the heat.
Rat made cocoa.

It snowed and snowed.
THUMP!
Someone was at the door.
"It's me," said a voice.

Rat opened the door.

It was Badger.

"I got lost trying

to get home,"

he said.

The door

opened again.

It was Skunk.

"I went out to buy flashlights and groceries.

It's impossible to go any farther.

Here," he said. "I'll share."

Skunk put the bags on the counter.

"Come on, little dumplings,
  you'll be safe and warm in here."
  Mother Hen walked in with her chicks.
  "We were on our way to
  Grandmother's house.
  We got stuck in the storm."
  She set a basket of food on the counter.

Next, the hockey team tumbled in.
"We were supposed to sing
in the Christmas concert,"
said a rabbit. "It was canceled."
A few members of the band
followed close behind.

"Oh look, a party," said Weasel.

"I'm glad I came.

Every other place in town is closed.

Do you have anything good to eat?"

"Can we have a party?" asked Badger.

"I don't see why not," said Duck.

7. The Party

It did not take long to set things up.

The hockey team began to sing.

The rest of the crowd sang along.

Then they danced.

After that it was time for the feast.

There was pumpkin soup, cheese and crackers,

salad, carrot cake, nuts, and gingerbread cookies.

Duck and Rat took turns reading
their favorite Christmas stories.
One story was happy.
Another story was mysterious.
The last story made everybody laugh.

Outside, the wind kept howling.

The snow piled up.

"No one is going anywhere tonight," said Duck.

"What about Santa?" asked the little chicks.

"Santa will be late this year,"

said Mother Hen.

She sang a lullaby.

Soon everyone was sound asleep.

In the middle of the night, Duck
thought he saw a stranger walk in.
"I must be dreaming," he said,
and went back to sleep.
Finally the snow tapered off.
The wind stopped.
It was morning.

"Hey, everyone, wake up," said Little Peep.
"Santa's been here!"
The front counter had rows of stockings
in all shapes and sizes.

Each one contained little presents
including oranges, nuts, a small toy,
a notebook, a pencil, and a book.
Skunk gave everyone cinnamon bread.
Badger passed around a fruitcake.
Then they all went outside.

"It's like millions of sparkles have been tossed to the ground," said Mother Hen. The hockey team swept the powdery snow into the air.

At that moment, a gust of wind caught the twinkling snowflakes and sprinkled them over the windowpane.

"LOOK!"

Everyone's eyes opened wide.

There in the window

stood a brand-new gingerbread house.

Etched in the ice and snow covering

the glass were the words

Merry Christmas
to
Duck & Company
from Santa

All the little chicks gathered around
Duck and Rat.
They gave their ankles great big hugs.
"We've had the best time ever,"
said Little Peep.

"We should do this again next year,"
said Weasel.